The Dreamy Adventures of a Shiny Nosed Bear

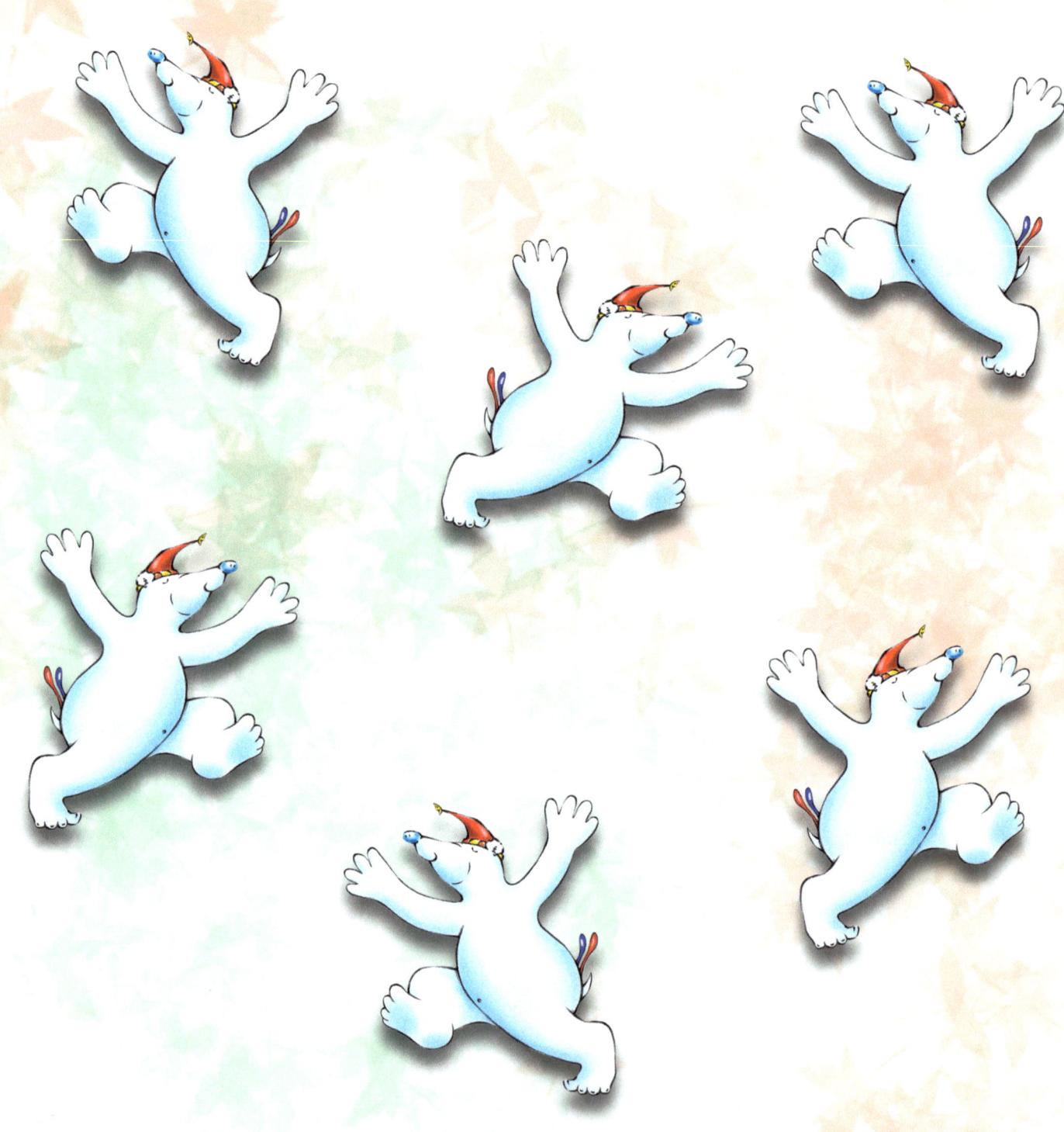

For Jack & Dylan.

Published by Peter Tasker.
First published in paperback in 2017.
ISBN 978-1-9999054-0-8

www.taskerdesign.com

DON'T DANCE ON THE CROCODILES

Written & Illustrated by

Peter Tasker

It was a quiet sunny Sunday morning, and Snoozer *the bear was doing what he does best.*

With a *twitch* of his shiny nose, he sniffed the *lovely* smell of his favourite treat

.... *mmmmmmmmm* .....

what a tasty thought.

The smell seemed to be coming through a hatch in the wall.
He'd never noticed a hatch there before, *how strange.*

Half asleep, he followed his nose and climbed in.
It was a tight squeeze, but the smell just got
stronger and stronger.

He wiggled and jiggled and
squeezed in even further, then just
as he thought he was through -
Uh-oh... he got well and truly stuck.

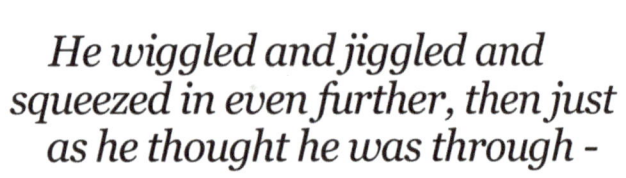

"Help, help, help!" he shouted,
"someone give me a push!"

"YES, YOU! give him a push!"

He landed with a **GREAT BIG** 'HECKY THUMP'

Animals and birds *Scampered*
away as dust and leaves flew into the air.

Luckily for *Snoozer* he landed on
something really nice and soft.

"Where on earth am I?
*This looks like an African jungle...
... and it's a bit scary!"*

The sound of animals
Roarrring, Screeeaching and
OOH-OOH-OOHING was everywhere.

With lots of trees and funny looking flowers,
BIG, small and *very, very small*
insects crawled and flew about, humming and
buzzing away to themselves.

As the jungle got thicker, darker and even more **scary,** *Snoozer's* ears pricked up when he heard something moving on the other side of a **humongous** brown bush.

Was it a hungry lion, looking for lunch?
Or an **angry alligator** with big sharp teeth?

Quietly peeking through the bush, he heard

a Great Big Loud ···

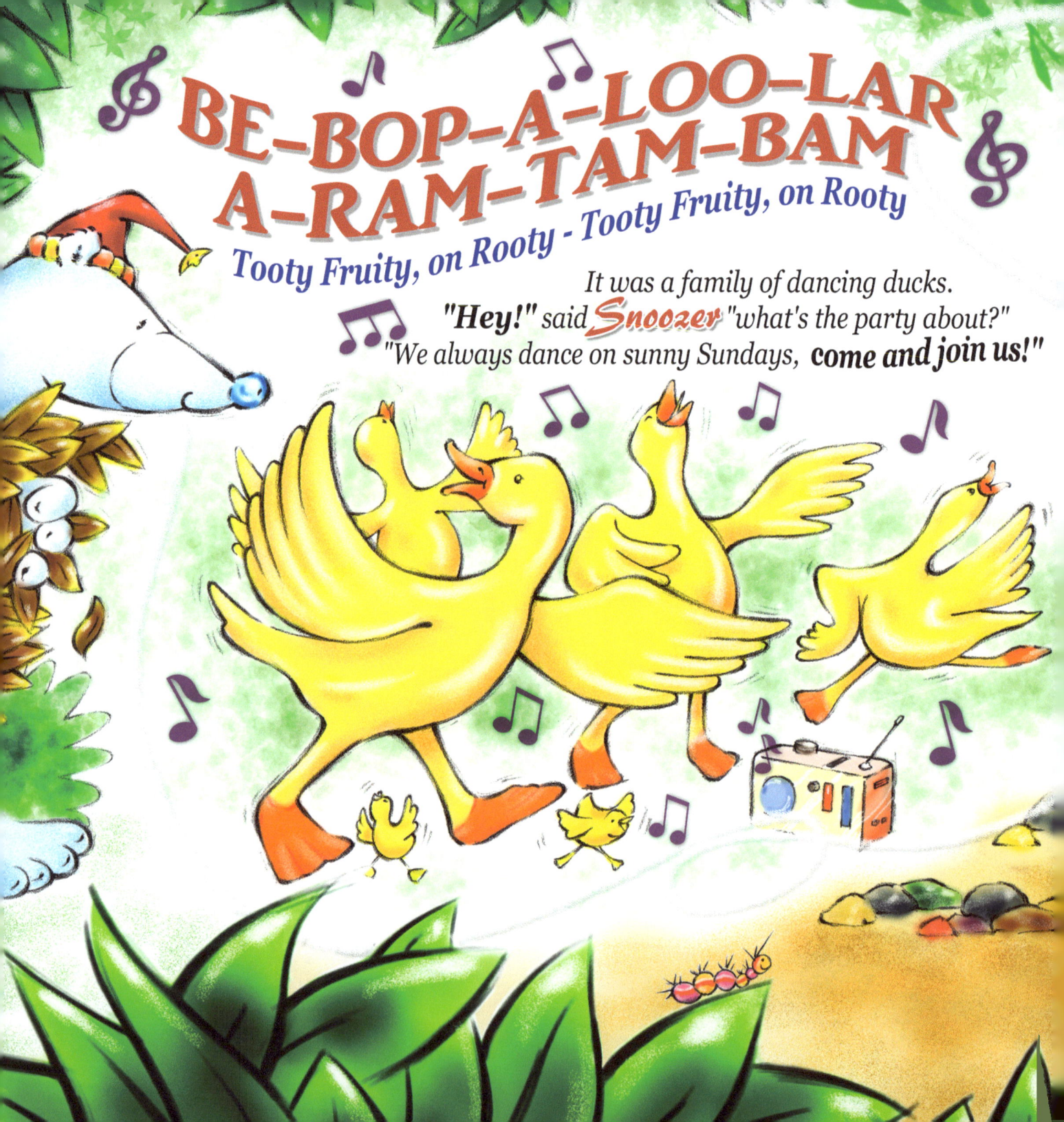

He **jumped** in the air and started to **jiggle and bounce** about shaking his bum like Billy-O with a

BE-BOP-A-LOO-LAR A-RAM-TAM-BAM

He was having so much fun that he didn't hear the ducks shouting ...

CROCODILES SNOOZER!"
at this time of the day!"

He stopped for a second and realised he was in the middle of a pond, dancing on some very unhappy snappy crocs.

SNAP - SNAP

He soon started bouncing higher as, SNAP - SNAP, he just made it, SNAP - SNAP, to the other side before...

SNAP - SNAP - SNAP - SNAP.

Pheeewww!

That was close.

"Help! Help! Help!"

He heard a little voice trying to **shout loudly**.

As he looked closer he saw a small
bumble bee all tangled up in an old spiders web.

"Looks like you need a hand,"
he said, and gave him a tug.

"Help! Help! Help!"

"Thank you!" said the little bee,
his face covered in pollen.

"Oh that's okay," *Snoozer*
replied, "I got stuck earlier
as well. What's your
name?"

'Co-Co Nut
Wobbly'

'The MEGA Mix'

'Ice Lolly Baby'

'Cherry Spaceship'

WHAT'S YOUR FAVOURITE?

'Ice Rocket'

'Vanilla Moon'

'Zebra Stripes Special'

"My name is B-Bee. What are you doing in the jungle?" B-Bee asked *Snoozer*
"I'm following a delicious smell," **Snoozer** said. "It's my ***favourite*** treat."

B-Bee buzzed a bit as he scratched his tiny head. **"I know"** he said, "that smell could be coming from the *'Jolly Lolly'* ice cream parlour." "They have lots of tasty flavours like vanilla, bo-nana, co-co nut and loads more, come on, I'll show you!"

They were just about to set off
when *Snoozer* felt a tap on his shoulder.

"HOLD IT RIGHT THERE!"
Came a loud angry voice.

"Are you the one they call *Snoozer*? I've been looking for
you **everywhere!**"

It was a very large elephant,
with a very long trunk.

"When you landed in the
jungle, you fell on top of
Sneaky Snake!"
he said.
"I've been trying to catch
him for pulling

too many tongues
at everyone,

and if it wasn't for you
he'd still be on the loose!"

"Jump on my back, and B-Bee can
show us the way to the *'Jolly Lolly'* for some
Extra Special ice cream as your reward,
it's *Delish!*"

At last they reached the *'Jolly Lolly'* with all sorts of animals enjoying their Sunday ice cream. *Snoozer* was **soooooo hungry** by now, and decided to have the *'Special of the Day'*.

A **HUGE** Rainbow Vanilla Swirl, with chocolate chip sprinkles, and sweet strawberry sauce topping,

- *Fit for a King.*

With one last lick of ice cream left on his spoon, *Snoozer's* tummy was **SO FULL** he thought his belly button might just

pop off.

When suddenly out of nowhere...

There was a **GREAT BIG CLAP OF THUNDER**
that made the whole jungle rumble and shake.
The heavens opened and it
Absolutely Poured Down

Ice cream flew **All** over the place,
making a right mess **everywhere**
as they all dashed around trying
to get out of the rain.

"That's good luck" **Snoozer** said,
as he dived into a tree hole
which looked a bit like the hatch
in his wall - *how strange!*

But with his belly so full after eating
all that ice cream ...

Yep!

He got well and truly stuck
all over again.

"Give him another
push someone!"

With a quiet little **bump** he landed back on his favourite cushion, nice and soft and *warm.*

"*Hecky Thump* what a busy day,"
he said as he gave a great big yawn.
"I'm so tired, I feel like a little snooze."

Then with one last sniff in the air
Snoozer fell fast asleep and
whispered, **"Good night, sleep tight,
don't let the Crocodiles bite!"**

Further contact and new book details at www.taskerdesign.com
Available from Amazon.com and other online book stores.

ISBN 978-1-9999054-0-8